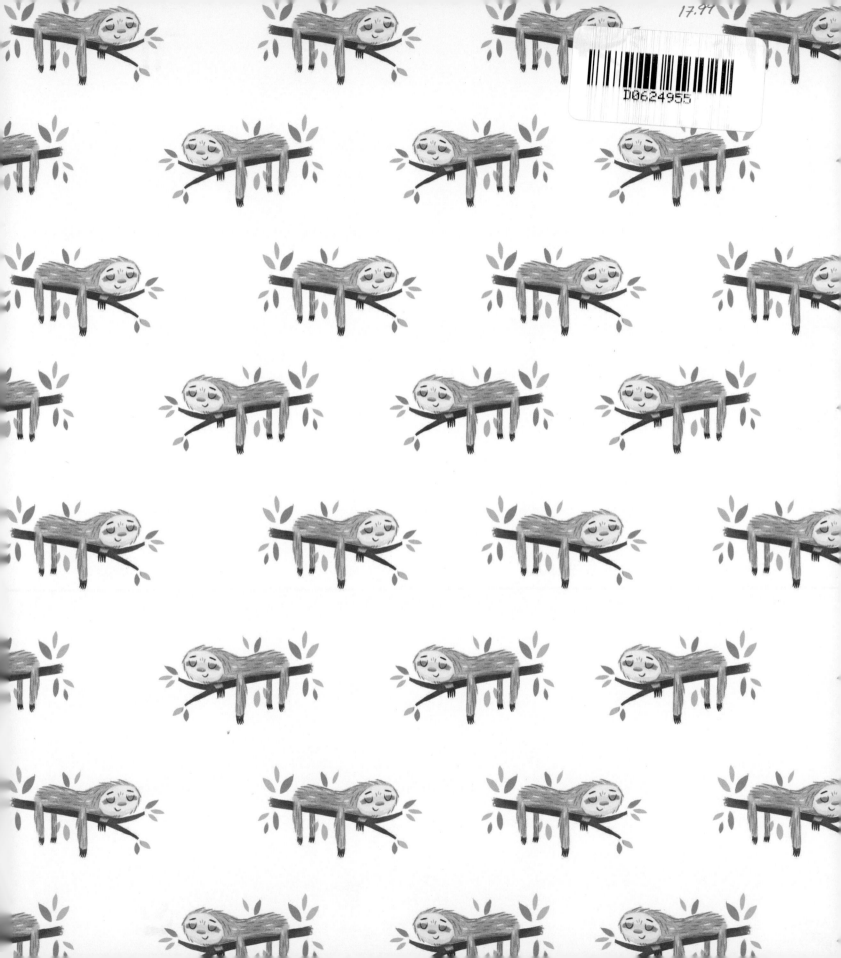

SLOTH TO THE RESCUE

by Leanne Shirtliffe

Illustrated by Rob McClurkan

RP|KIDS

PHILADELPHIA

**FOR VIVIAN, THE BEST DAUGHTER
AND BETA READER EVER.**
—L.S.

**FOR CASSIDY, HOUSTON,
AND THEIR AMAZING FRIENDS.**
—R.McC.

Running Press Kids
Hachette Book Group
1290 Avenue of the Americas, New York, NY 10104
www.runningpress.com/rpkids
@Running_Press

Printed in China

First Edition: October 2019

Published by Running Press Kids, an imprint of Perseus Books, LLC, a subsidiary of Hachette Book Group, Inc.

The Hachette Speakers Bureau provides a wide range of authors for speaking events. To find out more, go to www.hachettespeakersbureau.com or call (866) 376-6591.

The publisher is not responsible for websites (or their content) that are not owned by the publisher.

Print book cover and interior design by Frances J. Soo Ping Chow.

Library of Congress Control Number: 2018935980

ISBNs: 978-0-7624-9159-9 (hardcover), 978-0-7624-6334-3 (ebook), 978-0-7624-6630-6 (ebook), 978-0-7624-6631-3 (ebook)

1010

10 9 8 7 6 5 4 3 2 1

Sloth loves everything about Patti's visits.

His favorite everything is how
Patti isn't in a rush to see the big, loud animals.

She isn't in a rush to do anything,
except sit herself near Sloth's home away from home
and pull out her notebook.

Sloth likes looking at Patti's drawings.
And Sloth loves being the star of Patti's story.

One Saturday at the end of summer,
Sloth sees Patti's notebook, all alone.

He arrives at the notebook on Monday.

Oh. no, Sloth thinks.
Today. is. Patti's. first. day. of. school!

Sloth needs help. If he leaves today for Patti's school,
she'll be in eighth grade by the time he arrives—
without her notebook.

Sloth takes a big belly breath.
He remembers that he can ask for help, so he calls to his friends.

Sloth says, "Let's. go . . ." Peccary is always up for a morning trek.

". . . on. a. field. trip . . ." Boa likes fields.

". . . to. school. . . ." Capuchin enjoys big groups.

". . . Will. you. be. nice . . ."
Ocelot hears *will you eat mice*, so he's game.

". . . and. help. me?"

So, Sloth and his friends take a field trip to Patti's school.

The animals stop in their tracks.
They've never been to school before. It's big. And scary.

Sloth takes two big belly breaths.
He remembers that sometimes the best way
to calm down is to keep busy.

Sloth asks Peccary to help search for Patti in the schoolyard.

"Because. you're. good. at. lining. up."

Peccary fits right in. She says, "It's like we're traveling on a trail through the jungle!"

Sloth nods and slowly scans the schoolyard.
Nope, he thinks. *No. Patti. here.*

Sloth asks Boa to help search for
Patti in the coat room.

"Because. you're. good. at. removing. your. outer. layer."

He says, "It's like we're shedding our skins!"

Sloth nods and slowly scans the coats.
Nope, he thinks. *No. Patti. here.*

Sloth asks Capuchin to help search for Patti in the classroom.

"Because. you're. good. at. listening. to. the. leader."

Capuchin fits right in.

She says, "It's like we're grooming each other under
the watchful eye of the alpha female!"

Sloth nods and slowly scans the desks.
Nope, he thinks. *No. Patti. here.*

Sloth asks Ocelot to help search for Patti in the gymnasium.

"Because. you're. good. at. running."

Ocelot fits right in.

He says, "It's like we're playing in the jungle!"

Sloth nods and slowly scans the gym. *Nope*, he thinks. *No. Patti. here.*

Sloth slumps.
No. Patti. anywhere.

Sloth takes three big belly breaths. He remembers that sometimes the very best way to calm down is to take. his. time.

Then he notices her.

Because Sloth knows a dawdler when he sees one.

The animals stay for story time.
Patti opens her notebook and begins to read:

"Sloth loves everything about Patti's visits.
His favorite everything is how Patti isn't in a rush. . . ."

ANIMAL (AND HUMAN) FACTS

PECCARIES often walk in single file because it's easier to trek through the jungle when there's a path worn by other feet. That's why it looks like they're lining up.

One of the reasons that **BOA CONSTRICTORS** and other snakes shed is because their skin does not grow as they become bigger.

CAPUCHIN monkeys are highly sociable animals. They live in groups of 10 to 30, listen to the alpha, and groom each other.

The strong claws of **OCELOTS** help them climb and run quickly.

SLOTHS move so slowly that algae sometimes grows on their backs. This green coloring helps them camouflage among tropical trees. Licking the algae even gives them nutrients.

Most **CHILDREN** (and **TEACHERS**!) are nervous for their first day of school. Taking big belly breaths, asking for help, keeping busy, and slowing down are strategies that can help them feel better.

ANIMAL RESCUE CENTERS help protect hundreds of species. Whenever possible, animals are returned to their natural habitat.

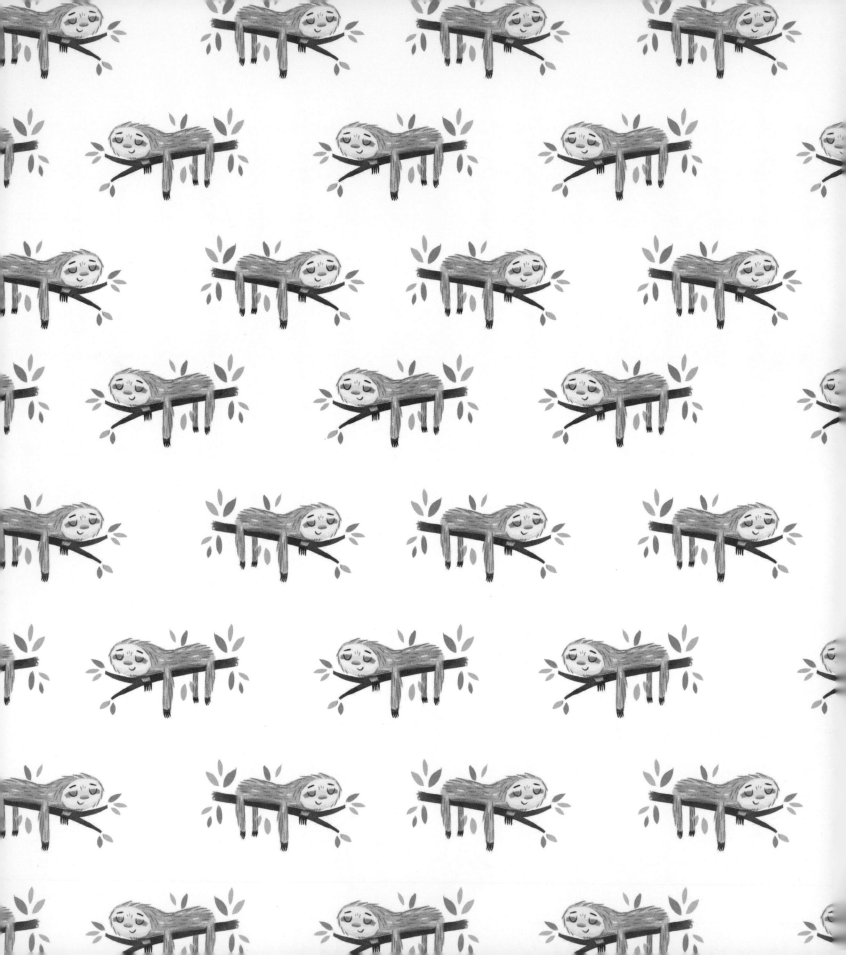